Miranda to the Rescue

Karen Wallace
Illustrated by Ailie Busby

A & C Black • London

To Evan and his fish, with love

www.acblack.com

Text copyright © 2010 Karen Wallace
Illustrations copyright © 2010 Ailie Busby

The rights of Karen Wallace and Ailie Busby to be identified
as the author and illustrator of this work has been asserted by them
in accordance with the Copyrights, Designs and Patents Act 1988.

ISBN 978-1-4081-1445-2

A CIP catalogue for this book is available from the British Library.

This book is produced using paper that is made from wood grown in
managed, sustainable forests. It is natural, renewable and recyclable.
The logging and manufacturing processes conform to the
environmental regulations of the country of origin.

Printed and bound in Singapore by Tien Wah Press (Pte) Ltd.

Chapter One

Miranda was a mermaid who lived on a big flat rock. Every day, while the other mermaids combed their hair and sang songs in high voices, Miranda painted pictures on seashells.

While the other mermaids wiggled their tails and waved to sailors, Miranda read books about underwater adventures.

"Don't you ever read fairy tales?" they asked, combing their hair and wiggling their tails. "This is what mermaids are *supposed* to do."

"I don't believe in fairy tales," said Miranda. "Besides, sitting around all day is a waste of time."

The other mermaids turned
away and shrugged their
pretty shoulders.

Who would fall for a mermaid with
short hair anyway?

Miranda had two friends.
One was an octopus called Malcolm,
who lived in a rusty tumble dryer.
Malcolm was always making things
from odd bits he found on the seabed.

Miranda's other friend was a dolphin
called Delia.
Delia used to live in a pool at the zoo.
Every day, she taught herself a new fact
as she swam backwards and forwards.

Now there was almost nothing Delia
didn't know, and she *loved* talking.

Chapter Two

One morning, Miranda was sitting
in her cave reading a book. Delia was
talking, and Malcolm was making an
underwater spyglass.

"When I was in the zoo," Delia was saying, "I saw thousands of faces every day. The fact is, there are good faces and bad faces."

Miranda looked up. "What do you mean?"

"Beady eyes and a mouth like a knife blade," said Delia firmly. "Those people were the worst. Even the sharks didn't like them."

"Jumping jellyfish!" cried Malcolm.
He passed the spyglass to Miranda.
"I don't believe it!"

Miranda held the spyglass to her eye.
A man in a suit was standing on the
mermaids' rock...

He had beady eyes and a mouth like a knife blade! And he was holding a sign. Miranda watched as he banged the sign into a crack in the rock. Then she passed the spyglass to Delia.

CRUSHED CORAL DREAM HOMES

For the first time, Delia's mouth opened but no words came out!

Chapter Three

"What are you going to do?" asked
Malcolm.

"Find out what's going on," said
Miranda, looking tough. "No one's
building dream homes on *our* rock."

"What if he sees you?" asked Delia.
She shuddered. "Remember, I told you
people like him are the worst kind."
"He won't see me,"
said Miranda, boldy.
"I'll go in disguise."

Ten minutes later, Miranda swam to the other side of the rock. She was wearing a spotty grey coat, and a dark green wig.

CRUSHED
CORAL DREAM
HOMES

15

Miranda crouched down behind a boulder. She looked just like a pile of pebbles with some seaweed on top!

Miranda watched as the man drew a picture of two houses on a flat rock.

He wrote "Paul and Patsy" on the door of one house, and "Stacy and Steve" on the door of the other. Then he took out a mobile phone, made two calls and said the same thing both times:

What on *earth* was he up to?

Miranda thought hard as the man jumped into a motorboat and roared away. Delia was right, the ones with beady eyes and a mouth like a knife blade *were* the worst kind!

Chapter Four

She rushed back to the cave to tell her
friends the news.
"This Gus Grabbit
must be stopped!"
cried Delia.

"How?" asked
Malcolm,
pulling a face.

"We need to make a plan." Miranda
sat down. "Any ideas?"
"I'll write a song so his boat gets stuck on
the rocks," said Delia. "He won't be able
to resist the mermaids' singing."

"And I'll make a goop gadget," said Malcolm.

"What's that?" asked Miranda.
Malcolm waggled his beak. "Something full of goop that makes a big mess."

"Perfect," said Miranda with a grin. "We'll give Gus Grabbit a welcome he'll never forget!"

Chapter Five

Later, Miranda gathered all the other mermaids together and showed them the drawings on the rock.

At first, they didn't understand the problem.

"What's wrong with a dream home?" asked a mermaid.

"Yeah," said another. "I'd like to live in one."

"He's not building the houses for you," explained Delia. She pointed to the names on the doors. "He's building them for *these* people."

"And you can bet your fins, they'd put you in a big glass box if they saw you." The mermaids gasped. "You mean like your pool in the zoo?"
Delia nodded her huge head, sadly.

PAUL + PATSY

STACY STEVE

All the mermaids started sobbing and pulling their hair.
"Boo! Hoo! Hoo!" they howled. "What are we going to do?"

"Help us get rid of them," said Miranda. "If we all work together, they won't have a chance."

She walked up to a flip chart made of bits of old sail and drew an enormous motorboat on it. She put a man with piggy eyes and rubbery lips on the deck.

"This is Gus Grabbit," said Miranda. "And he's bringing bad people to live on your rock. Tomorrow, he's having a party to celebrate."

There was a big silence as the mermaids thought about this. They stopped sobbing and twisting their hair.
"NO WAY!" they yelled.

"Excellent!" cried Miranda. "Now, listen carefully. This is my plan."

Chapter Six

The next morning, Miranda sent out a message on Malcolm's underwater radio. "Calling all jellyfish!" she cried. "Come to the mermaids' rock at six tonight."

Malcolm was busy making his goop gadget. He stuck a wheel to the side of an enormous tube and spun it with his eight arms. The tube sucked up lots of sandy goop and squirted it out of the top.

"Perfect," cried Miranda. "Malcolm! You're a genius!"

On the rock, Delia was busy teaching
the mermaids her special song.
She raised her flippers.
"One … two … three … go!"

"Gus Grabbit! The man of the moment!
Gus Grabbit! The king of the sea!
Gus Grabbit! So clever and handsome!
Come over and party with me!"

Miranda burst out laughing.
No one would be able to
resist them!

Chapter Seven

It was almost six o'clock.
Miranda was sitting on the rock in her
spotty coat and seaweed wig, watching
out for Gus Grabbit's motorboat.
Beside her was a
large curly shell.

When Miranda saw the boat, she blew through the shell and the mermaids began to sing.

Gus Grabbit followed the sound, and within seconds his boat was stuck on the rocks.

"What's going on?" snarled the people on deck. "We don't see no dream homes."

Gus Grabbit put down a gangplank
and led them ashore.
"Where are our dream houses?"
shouted the men.

Gus Grabbit pointed to the drawing on the rock. "Here. But I haven't built them yet, because I need your money first."

Miranda picked up the curly shell and
blew into it for the second time.
At the signal, Malcolm spun the wheel
of his goop gadget.

Splat! *Splat*! *Splat*!

"Yuck!" cried the women. "This is disgusting!"

"We'll wash it off in the sea," shouted the men. "Then we'll get out of here!"

Miranda blew into the shell for the third time, and thousands of jellyfish floated up through the water.

"JELLYFISH!" screamed the women. "What are we going to do?"

Creak… Creak… Creak…
Gus Grabbit was trying to push his boat
off the rocks and escape!
"GET HIM!" yelled the men.

Chapter Eight

After that, everything happened very quickly. One man grabbed the sign and whacked Gus Grabbit over the head.

The other grabbed his ankles.

The women pushed the boat free.
Then they shoved Gus Grabbit over
the side.

"Don't leave me!" he screamed. "There's nothing here but a lousy rock!" He grabbed hold of the motorboat as it roared away.

And from that moment on, the mermaids swore they would never sing songs or waggle their tails at sailors ever again.

Miranda was right! That kind of stuff *should* only happen in fairy tales.